Kes Gray & Nick Sharratt

Peas&Tickles

Double Daisy: Peas and Tickles
A RED FOX BOOK 978 1 782 95150 6

EAT YOUR PEAS
First published in Great Britain by The Bodley Head,
an imprint of Random House Children's Publishers UK
Text copyright © Kes Gray, 2000
Illustrations copyright © Nick Sharratt, 2000

YOU DO!
First published in Great Britain by The Bodley Head
An imprint of Random House Children's Publishers UK
Text copyright © Kes Gray, 2003
Illustrations copyright © Nick Sharratt, 2003

This collection first published as
Double Daisy: Peas and Tickles, 2013

1 3 5 7 9 10 8 6 4 2

Red Fox Books are published by Random House Children's Publishers UK,
61–63 Uxbridge Road, London W5 5SA

www.**randomhousechildrens**.co.uk
www.**randomhouse**.co.uk

Addresses for companies within The Random House Group Limited
can be found at: www.randomhouse.co.uk/offices.htm

THE RANDOM HOUSE GROUP Limited Reg. No. 954009

A CIP catalogue record for this book is available from the British Library.

Printed in China

The Random House Group Limited supports the Forest Stewardship
Council® (FSC®), the leading international forest-certification organisation.
Our books carrying the FSC label are printed on FSC®-certified paper. FSC
is the only forest-certification scheme supported by the leading environmental
organisations, including Greenpeace. Our paper procurement policy can
be found at www.randomhouse.co.uk/environment

Contents

**COLOUR FIRST READER books are
perfect for beginner readers.**

To Claire, Elliott and Jack – K.G.

To the Sullivans – N.S.

Eat Your Peas

It was dinner time again and Daisy
just knew what her mum was going
to say, before she even said it.
"Eat your peas," said Mum.

Daisy looked down at the little
green balls that were ganging up on
her plate.

"I don't like peas," said Daisy.

Mum sighed one of her usual sighs. "If you eat your peas, you can have some pudding," said Mum.

"I don't like peas," said Daisy.

"If you eat your peas, you can have some pudding and you can stay up for an extra half-hour."

"I don't like peas," said Daisy.

"If you eat your peas, you can have some pudding, stay up for an extra half-hour and you can skip your bath."

"I don't like peas," said Daisy.

"If you eat your peas, you can have ten puddings, stay up really late, you don't have to wash for two whole months and I'll buy you a new bike."

"I don't like peas," said Daisy.

"If you eat your peas, you can have 48 puddings, stay up past midnight, you never have to wash again, I'll buy you two new bikes and a baby elephant."

"I don't like peas," said Daisy.

"If you eat your peas, you can have 100 puddings, you can go to bed when you want, wash when you want, do what you want when you want, I'll buy you ten new bikes, two pet elephants, three zebras, a penguin and a chocolate factory."

"I don't like peas," said Daisy.

"If you eat your peas, I'll buy you a supermarket stacked full of puddings, you never have to go to bed again ever, or school again, you never have to wash, or brush your hair, or clean your shoes, or tidy your bedroom, I'll buy you a bike shop, a zoo, ten chocolate factories, I'll take you to Superland for a week and you can have your very own space rocket with double retro laser blammers."

"I don't like peas," said Daisy.

"If you eat your peas, I'll buy you every supermarket, sweet shop, toy shop, and bike shop in the world, seventeen swimming pools, you never have to go to bed again, or go to school, or wash, or brush your hair or clean your shoes, or clean your teeth, or clean your hamster out, or tidy your bedroom, or put the DVDs in yourself, or get dressed,

I'll buy you Africa and ninety-two chocolate factories, we'll move to Superland, you can have all the space rockets you want, I'll buy you the earth, the moon, the stars, the sun and . . . and . . . and . . .

...and a new fluffy pencil case!"

"You really want me to eat my peas, don't you?" said Daisy.

"Yes," said Mum.

"I'll eat my peas if you eat your Brussels," said Daisy.

Mum looked down at her own plate and her bottom lip began to wobble.

"But I don't like Brussels," said Mum.

"Exactly!" said
Daisy. "You don't
like Brussels and
I DON'T LIKE
PEAS!"

"But we both like pudding!"

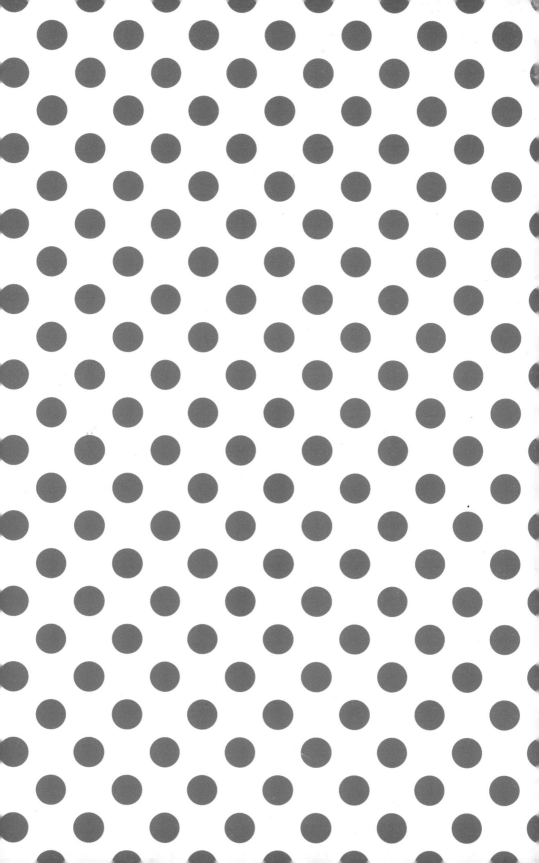

To Dennis, Nancy, Liberty
and Phoebe – K.G.

For Jessica and Emily – N.S.

You Do!

"Don't pick your nose," said Daisy's mum.

"You do," said Daisy.

"When?" said Daisy's mum.

"In the car on the way to Nanny's," said Daisy.

"I wasn't picking, I was scratching," explained Daisy's mum.

"Don't slurp your soup," said Daisy's mum.

"You do," said Daisy.

"When?" said Daisy's mum.

"On Saturday when we had chicken noodle," said Daisy.

"That's because I'd been to the dentist," explained Daisy's mum.

"Don't leave your clothes on the floor," said Daisy's mum.

"You do," said Daisy.

"When?" said Daisy's mum.

"Last week when you were going to that party," said Daisy.
"I couldn't decide what to wear," explained Daisy's mum.

"Don't wear your wellies in the house," said Daisy's mum.

"You do," said Daisy.

"When?" said Daisy's mum.

"Last weekend when you came in from the garden," said Daisy.

"That's because I had to fill the watering can," explained Daisy's mum.

"Don't keep fidgeting," said Daisy's mum.

"You do," said Daisy.

"When?" said Daisy's mum.

"In the church at that wedding we went to," said Daisy.

"That's because the seats were too hard," explained Daisy's mum.

"Don't sit so close to the telly," said Daisy's mum.

"You do," said Daisy.

"When?" said Daisy's mum.

"When you were watching that soppy film," said Daisy.

"I didn't have my contact lenses in," explained Daisy's mum.

"Don't talk with your mouth full," said Daisy's mum.

"You do," said Daisy.

"When?" said Daisy's mum.

"When your jacket potato was too hot," said Daisy.

"I wasn't talking, I was blowing," explained Daisy's mum.

"Don't lollop," said Daisy's mum.

"You do," said Daisy.

"When?" said Daisy's mum.

"Last Monday evening," said Daisy.

"I'd just done my exercises," explained Daisy's mum.

"Don't eat all the nice ones," said
Daisy's mum.

"You do," said Daisy.

"When?" said Daisy's mum.

"All the time," said Daisy.

"That's because I only like
the nice ones," explained
Daisy's mum.

"Don't keep saying **'you do'**," said Daisy's mum.

"You do," chuckled Daisy.

Daisy's mum put her hands on her hips and looked Daisy straight in the eye. "I do not keep saying 'you do', YOU DO!"

"You just said it **TWICE!**"
giggled Daisy.

"Right, who deserves a good tickling?" laughed Daisy's mum, chasing Daisy into the garden.

"I DO! I DO!"
squealed Daisy.